*For Holly, who created the first colorful sign,
and for Erik, who reminded us that not all creatures of
the night can read*
—J. R. J.

To Ereni, Gina, and George
—A. N.

SIMON & SCHUSTER BOOKS FOR YOUNG READERS
An imprint of Simon & Schuster Children's Publishing Division
1230 Avenue of the Americas, New York, New York 10020
Text copyright © 2019 by Jennifer Richard Jacobson
Illustrations copyright © 2019 by Alexandria Neonakis
All rights reserved, including the right of reproduction in whole or in part in any form.
SIMON & SCHUSTER BOOKS FOR YOUNG READERS is a trademark of Simon & Schuster, Inc.
For information about special discounts for bulk purchases, please contact Simon & Schuster Special Sales at 1-866-506-1949 or business@simonandschuster.com.
The Simon & Schuster Speakers Bureau can bring authors to your live event. For more information or to book an event, contact the Simon & Schuster Speakers Bureau at 1-866-248-3049 or visit our website at www.simonspeakers.com.
Book design by Krista Vossen
The text for this book was set in Sentinel.
The illustrations for this book were rendered digitally.
Manufactured in China
0319 SCP
First Edition
2 4 6 8 10 9 7 5 3 1
Library of Congress Cataloging-in-Publication Data
Names: Jacobson, Jennifer, 1958– author. | Neonakis, Alexandria, illustrator.
Title: This is my room! : (no tigers allowed) / Jennifer Richard Jacobson ; illustrated by Alexandria Neonakis.
Description: First edition. | New York : Simon & Schuster Books for Young Readers, [2019] | Summary: JoJo's first night in her own room is interrupted by a lion, then a bear, then a tiger and, while the first two obey her keep out sign, the tiger cannot.
Identifiers: LCCN 2017048129 (print) | LCCN 2017057893 (eBook) |
ISBN 9781534402119 (hardcover) | ISBN 9781534402126 (eBook)
Subjects: | CYAC: Autonomy—Fiction. | Literacy—Fiction. | Animals—Fiction. | Bedrooms—Fiction. | Bedtime—Fiction. | Sisters—Fiction.
Classification: LCC PZ7.J1529 (eBook) | LCC PZ7.J1529 Thi 2019 (print) | DDC [E]—dc23
LC record available at https://lccn.loc.gov/2017048129

THIS IS MY ROOM!
(NO TIGERS ALLOWED)

Jennifer Richard Jacobson

Illustrated by Alexandria Neonakis

Simon & Schuster Books for Young Readers
New York London Toronto Sydney New Delhi

"Tonight I'm going to sleep in my very own room in my very own bed," JoJo said.

"You'll be back," said Margaret.

"No, I won't," said JoJo. She skipped across the hall.

JoJo had just crawled under the covers, turned off the light, and stretched her toes from corner to corner in her very own bed when . . .

a lion slipped out from
behind the window curtain.

She could see the shadow of his mane on the wall. She could hear
the tuft of his tail *thump, thump, thump*ing against the baseboard.

She sat up quick and turned on the light.

The lion hid.

JoJo ran into Margaret's room.

"Back so soon?" asked Margaret.

"I'm not *back*, it's just that . . . there's a lion in my room."

"Well, then," said Margaret, "you need to make a sign."

Margaret helped JoJo find paper, a yellow marker, and flowered duct tape.

"Put them away when you come back," said Margaret.

I won't be back, thought JoJo.

JoJo wrote:

NO LIONS ALLOWED!

She taped the sign above her bed, crawled under the covers, and waited.

No lions allowed!

The lion, who no doubt read the sign, did not return. But then . . .

No lions allowed!

JoJo heard a bear. Its claws scritch-scratched across the floor.
She thought she smelled meatballs on its breath.

She ... ever ... so ... slowly leaned over and clicked on her light.

The bear hid.

JoJo jumped out of bed and raced into Margaret's room.

"I see you're back again," Margaret said.

"Now it's a bear!" said JoJo, who was *not* back.

"I need a brown marker."

She found the marker, mustered her courage, and stomped loudly across the hall (in case any bears were listening).

JoJo stood on her bed and wrote:
NO BEARS ALLOWED!

The bear, having no doubt read the updated sign,
did not return. But then . . .

A tiger crawled out of her closet, tripping over her shoes.

His nose twitched. He licked his lips.

JoJo held her breath and once again clicked on her light.

The tiger hid.

"I just need an orange marker!"
said JoJo, sprinting into the room.

She found it before Margaret
could say anything about
her being back.

JoJo stood up on her bed and wrote:

NO TIGERS ALLOWED!

"There!" she shouted. She wanted that tiger to know that in *her* room, *she* was the boss.

But when JoJo turned off her light,
the tiger slipped out from the closet again.

JoJo slapped her hands over her eyes.

Again JoJo turned on the light, but this time the tiger didn't bother to hide.

JoJo looked at the tiger. The tiger looked at her.

She looked at the tiger. The tiger looked at her.

JoJo thought of Margaret, snug in her bed in their old room, which was tiger-free.

But Jojo was *not* going back! She stood up on *her* bed, pointed to *her* sign, and shouted, "This is MY room! Can't you read?!"

The tiger squinted at the sign.

He shook his head back and forth, back and forth.

He made a sad tiger face.

Jojo paused. She pointed to the letters. "It says here, 'No tigers allowed!'"

But the tiger padded closer, and closer still. He reached out a paw.
JoJo covered her eyes again.

"Is this my letter?" he asked.

"Yes," said JoJo, peering out.

"That's *t* for Tiger."

Tiger smiled. "What's *this* letter?"
he asked, pointing to *N*.

"That's *n* for—"

JoJo stopped. She sighed.

"I'll show you from the beginning."

JoJo pulled out her very own alphabet book from her very own bookshelf and read to Tiger.

But the moon was high in the sky.

They only got to Tiger's *g*.

The next day, JoJo changed the sign in her very own room above her very own bed.

It read:

She was glad she did.